DISNEY
FROZEN

ADAPTED BY BILL SCOLLON

ILLUSTRATED BY THE DISNEY STORYBOOK ARTISTS

A GOLDEN BOOK • NEW YORK

randomhouse.com/kids

ISBN 978-0-7364-3065-4

Printed in the United States of America

On the edge of a fjord, a deep mountain lake ringed by majestic peaks, the kingdom of **Arendelle** was a happy place. During the day, shopkeepers, fishermen, and ice sellers kept the city bustling. At night, the northern lights often lit up the sky in beautiful patterns.

The rulers of Arendelle, the king and queen, were kind. Their young daughters, ELSA and ANNA, were the joy of their lives.

The older daughter, Princess Elsa, had a **MAGICAL SECRET**—she had the power to create snow and ice!

Anna adored her big sister and wanted to spend every minute with her.

One night, Anna convinced Elsa to turn the Great Hall into a WINTER WONDERLAND. They made a snowman together, and then Elsa created ice slides so Anna could soar through the air!

But Elsa accidentally hit Anna with a blast of icy magic. Anna fell to the ground, **shivering**. A streak of white appeared in her hair.

The worried king and queen rushed their daughters to the trolls. They were mysterious healers who knew all about magic.

A wise old troll was able to cure Anna by helping her to forget the injury—and the magic. He also had a warning. **"Elsa's power will grow," he said. "She must learn to control it."**

Elsa was afraid that she would hurt her sister again. She spent her time practicing to keep her magic under control. It was difficult, especially when she became upset. As a precaution, the king decided to keep the castle gates closed.

Anna couldn't remember Elsa's magic, but she still wanted to play with Elsa. **No matter how much Anna pleaded, Elsa refused to open her door.**

Years passed, but the girls didn't grow any closer, even when their parents were lost at sea. Then one summer day it was time to crown Elsa as queen. Guests from far away sailed to Arendelle for the coronation. Anna was excited to meet so many new people—especially a handsome young prince named HANS!

Meanwhile, Elsa was still struggling to hide her powers. She just hoped she could make it through the day.

Suddenly, bells rang. The ceremony was about to begin.

To Elsa's relief, the coronation went exactly as planned.

Afterward, a party was held in the Great Hall. Anna and Prince Hans spent the evening laughing and talking. IT WAS LOVE AT FIRST SIGHT!

Anna introduced Hans to Elsa—and announced that they were engaged.

Elsa objected. **"You can't marry a man you just met."**

"You can if it's true love!" Anna replied.

"My answer is no," Elsa said firmly, and started to leave the room.

Anna couldn't believe that Elsa was walking away without talking to her. Feeling upset, she grabbed Elsa's hand and accidentally **pulled off** her glove. "Why do you shut me out?" Anna asked.

"Enough!" Elsa cried. Suddenly, an icy blast shot from her uncovered hand—and coated the room in ice! Everyone stared in shock.

Frightened by her own power, Elsa fled from the hall. As she ran through Arendelle, everything froze around her. **"Stay away from me!"** Elsa warned her subjects. She didn't want to hurt anyone.

The townspeople were confused and afraid.
"Monster!" yelled the Duke.
Even the fjord froze as Elsa stepped onto the water.
All the ships were locked into the ice. Elsa quickly
crossed the fjord and ran up into the mountains.

As Elsa climbed higher, she let her powers loose. For the first time, she didn't have to hide them. She used her magic to create a beautiful ICE PALACE at the top of the mountain. It would be Elsa's new home, where she could be free—**and alone**. She'd never hurt anyone again.

Elsa's midsummer blizzard covered Arendelle with **snow and ice**. The whole kingdom was panicking, and Anna knew she had to find her sister.

Leaving Hans in charge of the kingdom, she rode into the mountains. But her horse got scared and threw her off. Anna was lucky to find a little trading post.

Inside the trading post, Anna bought dry clothes.
Just then, the door flew open. In came a mountain man
covered in snow. His name was KRISTOFF, and he said
that the storm was coming from the **North Mountain**.

That gave Anna an idea. She found Kristoff in the stable with his reindeer, SVEN. She asked him to take her up the North Mountain to find Elsa.

Kristoff agreed. **"We leave at dawn."**

"No," said Anna. "We leave right now."

As they headed up the mountain, Anna explained how her sister had started the storm. **And she told Kristoff about her true love, Hans.**

Suddenly, a pack of wolves began to chase them!
Working together, Anna, Kristoff, and Sven escaped
by crossing a deep gorge. But Kristoff's sled **crashed**
into the rocks below.

By dawn, they were almost at the top of the mountain. They looked down toward Arendelle, and it was covered with storm clouds. Here it was an icy wonderland.

"I never knew winter could be so beautiful," Anna said.

"But it's so white," added a voice. "How about some color? I'm thinking crimson or chartreuse . . ."

It was a living snowman!

"I'm OLAF," he said, explaining that Elsa had made him.

Anna asked Olaf to lead them to her sister. **"We need Elsa to bring back summer."**

Olaf grinned. "I've always loved the idea of summer," he said. "The warm sun on my face and getting a gorgeous tan."

"I'm guessing you don't have much experience with heat," said Kristoff, smiling.

"Nope," Olaf replied. **"Come on! Let's go bring back summer!"**

Olaf led Anna and Kristoff to Elsa's palace. **"Now *that's* ice!"** marveled Kristoff.

Anna told Kristoff and Olaf to wait outside. **"The last time I introduced her to a guy, she froze everything,"** said Anna.

Elsa was surprised to see Anna, and was
afraid of hurting her with her icy powers.
"You should go, Anna," Elsa warned.
"I'm too dangerous."
But Anna explained that Arendelle needed
her help. Elsa felt scared because she didn't
know how to unfreeze the kingdom.

Anna was sure they could figure it out together, but Elsa just grew more upset. Frustrated, she cried out, **"I can't!"**

An icy blast shot across the room and hit Anna in the chest!

Elsa hadn't meant to hurt Anna, and she worried she might accidentally do it again. **"Get out!"** she shouted, conjuring up a giant snowman.

The big snowman chased Anna, Kristoff, and Olaf to the edge of a cliff. They lowered themselves down, but the snowman grabbed the rope.

Desperate to escape, Anna cut the line!

Luckily, a blanket of snow cushioned the fall. Everyone was safe! But something was wrong with Anna. Her hair was turning white!

"What happened?" asked Kristoff.

"Elsa hit me with her powers," Anna replied.

Kristoff had an idea. **"We need to go see my friends,"
he said. "They can help."**

Night fell as they arrived in the realm of the trolls. Seeing Kristoff, their friend, the trolls came out of hiding.

An old troll said that Elsa had put ice in Anna's heart, which would make her freeze solid within a day. But there was still hope. "An act of TRUE LOVE can thaw a frozen heart," he explained.

Olaf and Kristoff decided to take Anna back home. Surely Prince Hans could break the spell with a true love's kiss.

Back at the kingdom, Hans had become alarmed when Anna's horse returned without her. So he rallied volunteers to find her.

Instead, Hans found the queen! Elsa tried to keep Hans and the others away from her. **But during the struggle, she was hit by falling ice and knocked unconscious.**

Kristoff brought Anna home to Arendelle castle. Servants whisked Anna inside. Kristoff was starting to realize that he cared deeply for Anna. But he knew she was in grave danger . . . **and she already had a true love.**

The servants brought her to the library, where she found a warm fire—and Hans!

Anna told him about the magic, and how his true love's kiss could break the spell.

"Oh, Anna," Hans said with a sneer. **"If only someone loved you."**

As he doused the fire, Hans explained that he had only been **pretending** to love Anna in order to take over Arendelle! All that was left, he said, was to get rid of Elsa. "Summer will return, and the kingdom will be mine!"

"You can't," gasped Anna as the ice slowly spread through her body.

Hans's search party had brought Elsa down from the North Mountain and imprisoned her in the castle. But while in the cell, Elsa's fears that she might hurt the kingdom had grown—and so had her magic. **Finally, her powers had burst through the walls.**

When Hans went to the queen's cell, Elsa was gone!

Meanwhile, Olaf had arrived just in time to help Anna escape from the castle. The little snowman realized that Kristoff loved Anna—which meant KRISTOFF'S KISS could break the spell!

Anna, nearly frozen, moved slowly across the fjord toward Kristoff. But then she saw something else. **Hans was about to strike Elsa with his sword!**

With all her remaining strength, Anna threw herself in front of Elsa. Hans brought his sword down just as Anna turned to solid ice. With a resounding **CLANK**, the blade shattered.

Elsa spun in surprise, then threw her arms around Anna's frozen figure. "Oh, Anna," she sobbed.

Suddenly, Anna began to THAW!

"Elsa?" whispered Anna, blinking.

"An act of true love can thaw a frozen heart!" Olaf said, suddenly realizing what had happened.

With her sacrifice, Anna helped her sister see that love was more powerful than fear. As Elsa's fear faded, love filled her heart and the winter snows began to melt.

After the fjord melted, the visiting ships sailed away. And Olaf was finally able to **enjoy summer**, thanks to a snow cloud that Elsa created for him!

Anna gave Kristoff a new sled, but he wasn't anxious to leave—especially when Anna surprised him with a KISS.

Elsa made an ice skating rink in the castle and threw open the gates. Everyone had a wonderful time skating with QUEEN ELSA and PRINCESS ANNA. At long last, the kingdom of **Arendelle was a happy place once more**.